Harriet,
You'll Drive Me Wild!

BY MEM FOX

ILLUSTRATED BY MARLA FRAZEE

HARCOURT, INC.

SAN DIEGO   NEW YORK   LONDON

To Wendy Bean, the Soft-Voice Queen
—MEM FOX

To my sister, Janel—transplendent amidst the Legos
—MARLA FRAZEE

Requests for permission to make copies of any part of the work should
be mailed to: Permissions Department, Harcourt, Inc.,
6277 Sea Harbor Drive, Orlando, Florida 32887-6777.

Library of Congress Cataloging-in-Publication Data
Fox, Mem, 1946–
Harriet, you'll drive me wild!/Mem Fox; illustrated by Marla Frazee.
p. cm.
Summary: When a young girl has a series of mishaps at home one Saturday,
her mother tries not to lose her temper—and does not quite succeed.
[1. Mothers and daughters—Fiction.   2. Clumsiness—Fiction.
3. Temper—Fiction.]   I. Frazee, Marla, ill.   II. Title.
PZ7.F8373Har   2000
[E]—dc21   98-11697
ISBN 0-15-201977-4

First edition
F E D C B A
Printed in Hong Kong

The illustrations in this book were done in pencil and
transparent drawing inks on Strathmore paper, hot press finish.
The display type was set in Minion Swash italic.
The text type was set in Adobe Caslon.
Color separations by Bright Arts Ltd., Hong Kong
Printed by South China Printing Company, Ltd., Hong Kong
This book was printed on totally chlorine-free Nymolla Matte Art paper.
Production supervision by Stanley Redfern and Ginger Boyer
Designed by Kaelin Chappell and Marla Frazee

*H*arriet Harris was a pesky child.
She didn't mean to be. She just was.

One morning at breakfast, she knocked over a glass of juice, just like that.

*H*er mother didn't like to yell, so instead she said,
"Harriet, my *darling* child."
"I'm sorry," said Harriet, and she was.

*A*t snacktime, she dribbled jam all over her jeans, just like that.

*H*er mother didn't like to yell, so instead she said,
"Harriet, my *darling* child. Harriet, you'll drive me wild."
"I'm sorry," said Harriet, and she was.

*B*efore lunch, when Harriet was painting a picture, she dripped paint onto the carpet, just like that.

Her mother didn't like to yell, so instead she said,
"Harriet, my *darling* child. Harriet, you'll drive me wild.
Harriet, sweetheart, what are we to do?"
"I'm sorry," said Harriet, and she was.

At lunch, Harriet slid off her chair and the tablecloth came with her, just like that.

Her mother didn't like to yell, so instead she said,

"Harriet, my *darling* child. Harriet, you'll drive me wild.

Harriet, sweetheart, what are we to do?

Harriet Harris, I'm talking to *you*."

"I'm sorry," said Harriet, and she was.

Later that afternoon, when Harriet was meant to be
napping, she ripped open a pillow, just like that.

$\mathcal{A}$ thousand feathers flew in every direction.

There was a terrible silence.

Then Harriet's mother began to yell.
She yelled and yelled and yelled.

"I'm sorry," Harriet cried. "I'm really, really sorry."

Her mother took a deep breath.

"I know you are," she said, hugging Harriet tight.

"I'm sorry, too. I shouldn't have yelled, and I wish I hadn't.

But sometimes it happens, just like that."

"Big mess," said Harriet.

"A *very* big mess," said her mother.

And she started to laugh.

$\mathcal{A}$nd they laughed and laughed and went on laughing as they picked up the feathers together.